A BIRD ON HER HEAD

AUTHOR
ROBERT ARNOLD

ILLUSTRATIONS
SUZANNE TILDEN-MORTIMER

A BIRD ON HER HEAD

Arcimboldo Publishing

ISBN | 9780578694078

Other children's books
by Suzanne Tilden-Mortimer

TAPPITY-TAP-Tap-TAP

HOUSES
Homes and Dwellings
Coloring book

MYRTA AND HER DOG WILLY

COLOR THE PAGES
WRITE THE STORY
A Children's Activity Book

COLOR THE PAGES
WRITE THE STORY
A Children's Activity Book 2

COLOR THE PAGES
WRITE THE STORY
A Children's Activity Book 3